# PONDERISMS

Looking at Life

Like You Never Thought

Possible or Necessary

Plucked From The Mind Of

Jack S T A R R

ISBN: 978-1-945975-03-5

Published by EA Books Publishing a division of
Living Parables of Central Florida, Inc. a 501c3
EABooksPublishing.com

# PREFACE

I was daydreaming at my desk one day, and my mind was wandering. (It does this frequently but always seems to return.) I thought, "What does it mean to 'shoot your mouth off'?" And I took that to many, many different levels as you can imagine—or not.

So when my rest period was over, I thought about other things like that which could make a person think, wonder, or just amuse themselves with for a period of time.

It sort of went from there. Being left handed, I had no trouble coming up with over fifteen hundred of these wonderments. And then I pondered, "What should I call them?" I think you can guess the answer to that.

When I asked some of my friends about this

word, they looked at me as if to suggest that I had lost my mind. Now I have lost some marbles in my life, but not my mind. They were not too supportive of me in this project, but I trudged on, alone, day and night . . . rain, sleet, and snow . . . until I came to the conclusion that they were not going to help encourage me.

In fact, one day, some men in white coats came to the door, but I said I wasn't home. Not sure what they wanted. They put their jacket and stretcher back in their white van and drove away. They never came back. And I continued.

The results are included in this book. I have more . . . many more. I could do a sequel, but I think I will wait for the movie to come out before I produce a follow-up. More money, I think.

So I urge you to read on and discover for yourself the wonderment of abstract, off-the-wall and out-of-the box thinking. It will not make your day more profitable, filling, or enlightening, Go Ponder!

# FOREWORD

*"I am pleased to be asked to write the foreword to the first book on Ponderisms.*

*I have known the author, Jack Starr, for his entire life or so it seems, He was an average child, oldest of 3 siblings, and was the Starr of his high school football team. He started out college in journalism and then went to medical school at Ohio State. He said he 'played doctor' in London, Ohio as a family physician for 37 years. Currently he is still a hospice physician and actually makes house calls,*

*He is married to his current wife, Wendy (33 years) and between them have 12 kids (10 for Jack and 2 for Wendy).*

*He has always enjoyed kidding around and especially liked being a doctor to children. He would often say to them "Now if you don't get better with this medicine, next time we will have you see a real doctor." Kids would say O.K. and Mom would frown, mutter, and finally smile.*

*He was an amateur magician since the 7th grade, enjoys cooking, gardening, traveling and currently has a trophy shop (for 30 years....15 years before he retired.) and can be found there, still making trophies and other awards.*

*He apparently got the idea for this book after a few days of boredom during which time he started jotting down some of these unusual ideas. Perhaps he gets these silly notions because he is left handed and so it is a given he is NOT in his right mind. ...or is he?*

*I can honestly say that he would be the last person to entertain the idea that he is talented, wise, or clever. He is always trying to 'think outside the box' and actually lives his life that way. You never know exactly what he is going to do or why. And so this book has evolved.*

*I will close with this. The world is more better for having had him around for all these years. Yes I said 'more better'. He always says that!"*

*A close anonymous friend.*

# INTRODUCTION

## PONDERISMS

PONDERISM is a word I coined. You will not find it in the dictionary. So I shall explain what it means. The verb ponder means to consider deeply and thoroughly, to weigh carefully, to meditate. With that in mind, it seems logical that the noun PONDERISM means something you wonder, analyze, consider carefully, or think about. Perhaps even worry about or just plain PONDER what in the world this or that all about. And you thought that there was nothing new under the sun.

You don't have to be an intellectual or genius to consider a ponderism. You just need a little curiosity or time on your hands. They will not make you more knowledgeable, prettier, or richer, but one fact for sure is they definitely are not fattening. (Unless you munch on snack food while you think.)

By now if you haven't skipped ahead in this book, you are probably curious as to just what I am talking about. Well, let us consider some of these mind-bending statements.

How much rope do you need to be able to tie a knot and hang on?

Now you can ponder just how long the rope should be, what kind of knot or how far down the rope it should be. Should there be more than one knot? How thick is the rope? If you're at the end of your rope, do you have enough to hang yourself? And what, in heaven's name, is the other end tied to? And so on.

You see how this one statement can cause you to dig deeper in order to make sense of it . . . or is there any sense to it? Do you really need to know? Will it make you a better person if you figure this out? See, you are now a ponderer, thinking about a ponderism. Wow. How does this make you feel? Let us consider some others.

At what age do you quit acting responsibly?

If you shoot a mime, should you use a silencer?

Very interesting topics. At what age do you start acting responsibly? Or with the mime, could you use a mime gun? What if the glass wall he's miming is bulletproof? You will have to decide that for yourself. But you can spend an entire afternoon mentally wrapped up in this.

Now before you throw this book away, take a few minutes and read more. It may not make you older and wiser, but it will definitely make you (a little) older.

Is it true that Adam's rib was the first bone of contention?

Very interesting, no? I'm sure you can ponder this for yourself without any suggestions from me. I have grouped some of these ponderisms logically so you can keep your mind from running to and fro—that's how you become scatterbrained.

# CONTENTS

# Foods

## CHOCOLATE PONDERISMS

Chocolate is a favorite of a majority of the ones who responded to this survey—one I took in my mind. It is fattening, but otherwise delicious. It can be found in many edible foods. (Is there any other kind?)

I could not find one adverse comment about chocolate (other than from diet pushers, and even they wish they could eat it). Read on and fantasize about this wonderful food.

If chocolate is the answer, does it matter what the question was?

You won't need therapy if you have enough chocolate.

A balanced diet is an equal amount of light and dark chocolate.

Heads I will eat chocolate, tails I will eat Hershey's.

Hang around people who don't like chocolate, especially on Valentine's Day, Easter, and Halloween.

Chocolate and heaven are very close together in my world.

My road to success is paved in chocolate.

If you were drowning in a sea of chocolate, would you want to be rescued?

You can find chocolate (as if I had to tell you) in cupcakes, pies, ice cream, cereal, cakes, chocolate-covered ants and grasshoppers (not bad actually), and candy of all kinds. There is no bad chocolate. No, really, there isn't.

I have a lot more of these chocolate sayings, but I got hungry for chocolate just writing about this, and now that I have eaten a lot, I am sleepy and need a nap. More later. ZZZZZ . . .

## FOOD PONDERISMS

Think about these. Some are true. Some are "WHAT?" Others are “Oh for goodness sake,” and others you can try and make some sense out of for whatever reason is important to you. GO PONDER!

Do employees at a tea factory get a coffee break?

Why is there no egg in eggplant and no ham in hamburger?

Instead of crying over spilt milk, why not just milk another cow?

If you can catch more flies with honey than vinegar, why would you want to?

Where does evaporated milk go?

## PIE-IN-THE-SKY PONDERISMS

You have heard the saying "pie in the sky." Well, let us take this into the world of Ponderisms. This is no half-baked idea either. Look at these and see how Ponderisms cook in my mind. Slice into these and see how they pan out.

What is a pie in the sky?

What flavor is a pie in the sky, blueberry?

Can you buy a pie in the sky in the Sky Mall catalogue?

Does pie in the sky have to be baked? What if it's only half baked?

What would you pay for a pie in the sky?

Is pie in the sky hard to swallow?

What does a pie in the sky taste like?

Will ice cream go well with a pie in the sky?

Does a pie in the sky need a parachute?

If there were cake in the sky, would it be angel food?

Now let's digest these for a while and move on to something else before our senses dessert us.

## EGG POND ERISMS

I do not egg-xactly know how to crack this subject other than to just lay it out there. Before I'm done, you might want to scramble out of here. But here goes.

If you have egg on your face, do you need a washcloth?

If chickens drank colored water, would they lay colored eggs?

Is a hard-boiled egg the same as a hard-headed person?

If you put all your eggs in one basket, how many would you have?

IF you break six eggs, will you have seven years of bad luck or a great omelet?

Do you get a cracked egg from a crackpot?

If you have eggs in your basket, are you coming from or going to the store?

Why does the Easter Bunny deliver chicken eggs?

Will a double-yolked egg become a double-minded chicken? Would it doublecross you?

Well, folks, I guess the yolk is on you if you take all this seriously. Who would have hatched the idea that you could make ponderisms about eggs? Well, I did. See, that is why I am writing this book and not you. Do you get it? Or am I going to get it?

## A SECOND HELPING OF FOOD PONDERISMS

Food makes for some wonderful ponderisms.

First of all, food is very colorful. There is WHITE vinegar, BLACK pepper, BROWN sugar, GREEN onions, RED peppers, ORANGES, YELLOW squash, PURPLE grapes, and BLUE-berries.

For an interesting afternoon, try to come up with as many different foods as you can for each color. Write them down and see which color has the most. Or which food comes in the most colors. (Easter eggs don't count.) This has nothing to do with ponderisms, but it helps pass the time on a boring afternoon.

How is whole wheat flour different from partial wheat flour?

Do bell peppers make noise?

Where does extra virgin olive oil come from? A leftover virgin?

If you beat an egg, will it charge you with child abuse?

Can sour cream spoil? How would you know?

If you mince your words, do they taste better?

Is the wheat germ contagious?

How much longer is regular bread than shortbread?

Remember, these are ponderisms. Think about each one and drill down in it until you come to the core or you run out of energy. Does reading about food ponderisms make you hungry? Ponder that!

# Animals

Fish Ponderisms

Dog and Cat Ponderisms

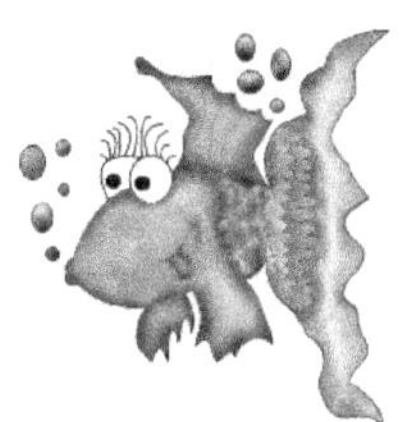

## FISH PONDERISMS

There are a lot of ponderisms you can think about with various animals. Let us see if we can enlighten you with a few about fish. Before looking at these, see if you can think of any.

Fish have a good life . . . they don't have to pay for food, clothes, gasoline, or traffic tickets.

Are fish dumb or more intelligent because they are usually in schools?

If you feel like a fish out of water, does that mean you are dry?

Do fish sweat? How would you tell? Fish must have good ears. Why else would fisherman need to be quiet in order to catch fish?

Do fish get out of school for holidays or weekends?

Do fish go home and tell everyone how big a fisherman they got away from?

There are many more of these. Send me some yours, and if I print them, I will give you credit. Not money, just credit.

## DOG AND CAT PONDERISMS

Dogs and cats are not archenemies as some would think. They occasionally will sleep together or even play together. Other times they fight like cats and dogs. What else would you expect?

### CATS

If cats are so clean, why are they covered with cat spit?

Why do only cats have nine lives?

Cats must be smarter than dogs because you can't get eight cats to pull a sled in the snow.

If a cat swallowed a ball of yarn, would the kittens be born in sweaters?

Would cats eat more if the food were mouse flavored?

If a cat is purring, it doesn't mean that he likes you.

Who owns your home, you or your cat? Really? Then why doesn't she have to move when you want to sit down? Cats won't fetch a rubber ball, but they'll play with a ball of yarn for hours.

## DOGS

Do blind dogs need a seeing-eye person?

What kind of watch does a watchdog wear?

Does a watchdog need coffee to stay awake all night?

If your dog likes television, does that make him a watchdog?

Your dog's licker does not come in a bottle.

Are you your dog's best friend?

If only your friends could be as loyal as a dog.

Dogs don't have hairballs. They take real baths.

Why do dogs chase cars? Wouldn't it be easier to catch a parked one?

What would a dog do if it ever caught a car?

Do people ever cremate their cats like they do dogs?

For those who own a dog (by the way, you can NOT own a cat .. They own you), once they get out of The puppy phases, they are wonderful. Puppies are also cute, but cause some problems as those of you know. The trouble with dogs, is that you can't leave them alone for several days like you can cats. Your house would

Smell really bad or worse . . . well you know. But Dogs offer companionship, are comforting, and a good Friend. They become a part of your family and honestly mind you better than your kids do or did.

# Professions

Doctor Ponderisms

Golf Ponderisms

Lawyer Ponderisms

Leader Ponderisms

## DOCTOR PONDERISMS

Doctors take good care of us. They check you, examine you, order tests, evaluate those tests, order more tests, prescribe medication, say, "Hummm" a lot, and wear white coats. Sometimes they drive fancy cars and take extravagant vacations when they're not relieving you of your pain, misery, and money. Notice how I slipped money in there. Why do we pay them so much when they are just practicing medicine? Don't they ever do it for real?

See if you agree with some of these ponderisms.

Do doctors take the oath of Hippocrates or the oath of the Hypocrites?

If a doctor's practice is in the mall, does he need mall practice insurance?

If your doctor is making a house call, does that mean he is going home for lunch?

If two doctors get together, do you have a paradox?

Did doctors who used to make house calls really have a baby in that little black bag? Isn't that what they meant when they said he "delivered" the baby?

Why do nurses always give the shots? Don't the doctors know how?

Is there a doctor who specializes in taking care of stupid people?

If a doctor operates on you, does he then know you inside and out?

Do doctors take a special pill each day to keep from getting sick?

Do internal medicine doctors only take care of diseases that are inside of people?

You can ponder these for quite a whilte, but the answer will still be the same. What is that? You let me know.

## GOLF PONDERISMS

Some wise old sage or old duffer once said, "Golf is a good walk spoiled." I think that was Mark Twain. But golfers are incredible people. They will tell you it never rains on a golf course and come home dripping wet. But they are persistent, persuasive, petulant, problematic, and diligent. (How did that word get in there?)

(Best read aloud:) Why do golfers shoot 5, yell "Fore," and write down 3?

Do golfers or fishermen tell the better lies?

A bad day of golf is . . . well, you know.

Par is considered average, but most golfers are not.

If you shoot your age, how many holes did you play? Really?

If you get a birdie, will you get arrested?

Did you ever miss a hole-in-one by three putts?

If you play scratch golf, does that mean you keep the good scores and scratch out the bad ones?

Golf Rule #10: Don't pick up a lost golf ball if it is still rolling.

Well before I get off this topic, I hope I haven't teed off any golfers. I do play golf, but not the game anyone would recognize. I have extra clubs in my bag. A foot wedge, a didn't-meant-it club, and a gimme club. I use these each and every game. They do not lower my score much, but I feel better having them along. My score is one of the best-kept secrets in this game.

## LAWYER PONDERISMS

My wife is a lawyer. I must be careful what I say here. So I will just get to the ponderisms.

Is there a menu for what is "court ordered"?

Ever wonder what kind of clothes a judge wears under his robe?

Since justice is blind, is that why courts have hearings?

If you get a jury of your peers, does a stupid person get twelve stupid people?

How committed do you have to be to commit perjury?

Does a jailhouse lawyer live there?

When a lawyer is at the bar, what kind of drink does he order?

If a case is overturned, how big a mess will it make?

If a lawyer gets a retainer, does he put it in his mouth or his wallet?

If a lawyer loses a case, does he look for it in the lost and found?

Well I hope I didn't exercise poor judgment on this topic, or else I may (1) not get supper (2) have to sleep on the couch, or (3) go to divorce court. Pick one or more.

## LEADER PONDERISMS

Being a leader is important if you are going to get where you want to go. Don't committee your decisions . . . make them even if they turn out to be wrong. Being indecisive is the worst thing anyone can do. And don't ever second-guess yourself.

You cannot lead from behind or by sitting on your behind.

Leading is putting your best foot forward before someone beats you to it.

A successful leader can tell if those behind him are following him or chasing him.

Leaders keep going where others' footsteps stop.

If you lead from behind, you can't see where you are going.

Leaders know the difference between going the extra mile and being lost.

Leaders know what to do when they come to what appears to be a dead end.

Leading is not something you learn, it is something you do.

Leading by the seat of your pants does not mean you are going backwards.

You can be a leader by yourself—if you're going the right way, others will follow.

Politicians seldom lead . . . By the time they have come out of committee, the opportunity to lead has passed. Don't be a politician, be a LEADER . . . not a follower . . . a LEADER!

# Man, Woman, Child

## PONDERISMS ABOUT MEN

Yes, there are ponderisms about women too. Keep looking. Men wear ties unless they are blue-collar workers or just don't care or their job does not make them wear a tie . . . or they are rebels.

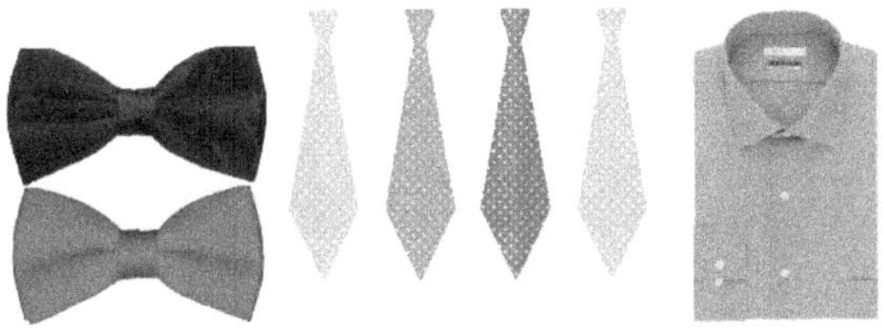

Do blue collars only belong to dogs? Watch how you ponder this.

The ideal husband can soon become the wife's ordeal.

Being a husband is like any other job. It helps if you like the boss.

If man evolved from apes, why do we still have apes?

A man is wise if he thinks twice before saying nothing.

Do you know of two small words that will cost a guy a small fortune? I do.

Weathermen are seldom right. Often they will say it's a 50% chance of rain. But if does rain, isn't that 100%?

If a guy had a close shave, did it have to involve a barber?

What happens when a double-minded man marries a two-faced woman?

Okay, all you men. Do any of these apply to you? Men think differently from women. Let me know how these played out in your life. I don't expect to hear from any of you.

## PONDERISMS ABOUT LADIES

Ladies, women, mothers, aunts, sisters, grandmothers, or wives, By what other name do we call a Rose? Flattering? Of course, how else do you think my wife would allow this to appear in print? Now the women in my life are special, since I have so many of them. A wife and ten girls. (Only two boys, and yes, that is a dozen. Glad you can do the math.) Ponderisms about them come in many flavors, but chocolate is the one women like best.

If you want a woman's advice and you ask for it, you had better follow it.

If you wife is always late, is that because her ancestors come over on the "June Flower"?

Women know that friends and family are more important than anything else in the world.

How much time is it really when a woman says, "I'll be ready in a minute"?

If a woman has a magnetic personality, is she at the North Pole?

If a lady's heart is broken, who picks up the pieces? What if they miss one?

A successful marriage is letting your wife be boss for the first 25 years. If you live that long, let her continue for the next 25.

If a woman works her fingers to the bone, she will never need a manicure.

To my wife, comfort food means chocolate.

He should not be your Prince Charming if he does not make you his princess.

Hooray for the ladies . . . if not for them, this world would be missing something. Kids, perhaps. So give your wife, girlfriend, or significant other a kiss and tell them how much you love them. You will see immediate results from this, I promise. Unless you are doing it for forgiveness. Watch out then, watch out.

## CHILDREN (KIDS) PONDERISMS

Children are a delight, a nuisance, a joy, a frustration, and a bowl of happiness and sadness all rolled into one. If you don't have children, or if your parents didn't have children, you will not understand what I am talking about. There are several profundities about these little rug-rats that are not meant to be mean spirited, but hopefully they will remind you why God gave these characteristics to young people. Here goes.

For an eternal optimist, nothing is impossible--except teenagers.

Answering a child's questions may be as difficult as tying your shoelaces with mittens on.

Grandkids are the gift God gives us for growing older.

Children are pencil sharpeners for a parent's mind.

A spoiled grandchild is a joy to grandparents who get to leave and go home.

Do teens suddenly "know it all," or does it happen slowly?

If it is Nerd Day at school, do your children want to borrow your clothes?

Be old enough to know the rules and young enough to break them.

We all are children at heart. How do you visualize yourself? As you are now? Or as you were when you were younger, like in high school? Are you thinner? With more hair? Or fewer scars? As we get older and older, we still think we can do those things we did when we were younger. In some cases, much younger. But the only consolation is that we get wiser as we get older . . . or I would hope so.

## PEOPLE PONDERISMS

These could be labeled PP, but then that would take you in a whole different direction. We are not ready for that yet.

Some people are good losers . . . the others can't act.

If people only talked about what they understood, would the silence be unbearable?

The weaker the facts, the stronger the opinions.

Some people make things happen; some watch things happen; others wonder what happened.

Can fat people go skinny dipping?

If people are not listening to you, is it because you are talking too softly or too much?

Be a Person . . . Don't be a People.

If you get together a bunch of people persons, are they people people?

Can you be dumb as a hay rake?

I just threw that last one in to see if you were paying attention. It has nothing to do with people. Well, it sort of does, I guess. Now that is the beauty of these ponderisms. At face value, they don't seem to make any sense, but in reality they are very thought provoking and worth thinking about . . . if you have time.

# Ponderisms and You

## YOU PONDERISMS

You are unique. You are important. You are one of a kind. Do you value yourself? Here are a few ponderisms that may reflect the you in you.

If YOU don't know what you are doing, don't encourage others to do it.

Do YOU say what you think, even if you don't think first?

If YOU rub someone the wrong way, is there a right way to rub someone?

How can YOU be dead right or dead wrong if you're alive?

If YOU are going to spend a day doing something, how much will it cost?

Are YOU the kind of person you would like to meet?

Can YOU be used for a good example or a bad one? How about an ugly one?

How would YOU know if you won the human race?

WOW! Aren't YOU wonderful? Or are YOU an afterthought? Or what if YOU were the only one left on earth? Why am I asking these questions about YOU? I thought this was all about ME. Who is the important one around here? HUH?

## YOUR LIFE PONDERISMS

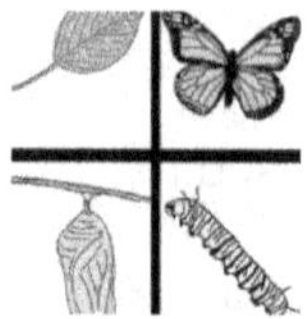

Life is to living as catepillar is to butterfly. Do you understand that? Well, I should hope so, for heaven's sake.

Life is a one-way ticket to eternity.

Why do stupid people always get stupid advice?

Is it your intention to live your life in order to create misery for others?

Is your life in black and white or in color?

The meaning of your life is hidden inside you.

Your life should not be controlled by a remote control.

Do you spend a lot of energy just trying to be normal?

Ever notice that when you change your mind, you're still stuck with the old one?

If you want to lead, get out in front. You can't lead from behind.

I thought about naming this section "food for thought," but then I wasn't hungry, so I left the food part out. Come to think of it, I left the thought part out as well. Now you know why I only get visitors on certain days.

## PROMISE PONDERISMS

We have been taught that it is important that we keep our word. Is that the same as a promise? We often promise things that we cannot possibly do. Is that okay? Here are some things to think about re: promises.

Is a promise an abstract thing until it becomes a reality?

Does a broken promise have sharp edges? It must, because it can hurt people.

If you keep a promise, where exactly do you keep it?

How long do you have to keep a promise? Does it ever spoil?

Does God keep score if you don't keep a promise?

Promise me this . . . promise me that . . . what is THIS and THAT?

Children always know if you keep your promise, but do adults?

Promises are those little secrets that we look forward to. Or is it vice versa?

I promise that I will not subject you to more ponderisms than you can ingest or digest. Oh, what the heck, I probably won't keep it anyway.

# Questions

Scratch Your Head Ponderisms

Stir The Pot Ponderisms

I Wonder Ponderisms

What If Ponderisms

Who Said Ponderisms

# SCRATCH -YOUR -HEAD PONDERISMS

Here are some ponderisms that make a whole lot of sense or make you scratch your head and worry what this generation is coming to.

Never let a fool kiss you and never let a kiss fool you.

Advice is like cooking; you need to try it yourself before feeding it to others.

For some people, cleanliness is not next to godliness, it is next to impossible.

Why is a fat chance the same thing as a slim chance?

Walking the talk is easier if you don't have a lot to say.

A flashlight is a case for storing dead batteries.

By now you make think, and perhaps correctly, that the author has either lost his mind or misplaced some if not all of his marbles. If you think his elevator does not go all the way to the top, perhaps it would make sense for him to take the stairs.

Some people are wise; the rest are otherwise.

Don't underestimate the value of doing nothing.

When you dial a wrong number, why do you never get a busy signal?

Two things on earth are universal: Oxygen and Stupidity.

Let's call fettuccini alfredo what it is: mac and cheese for adults.

Remember what they say about scratching your head. If your hand itches, you are going to get something. If your head itches, you got it.

## STIR-THE-POT PONDERISMS

Here are some fresh facts for the uninformed, misinformed, and malnourished. Try them on someone and see their reaction. Perhaps they will gain new respect for your insight and knowledge, or they may just throw up.

Pity a person who does not know how to read on a rainy day.

Never have a battle of wits with someone who is only half prepared.

You cannot stub your toe if you are standing still.

If evolution is true, why don't snakes have legs by now?

Here are some others that seemed to make sense a few minutes ago, but now not so much.

Do they use sterilized needles for lethal injections?

Why do kamikaze pilots wear helmets?

Some minds are like concrete: all mixed up and permanently set.

You can never find a lost opportunity.

Be thankful you can blow out the candles on your cake, even if it takes three tries.

Well, are you getting the drift of this? Or are you confused, disoriented, and annoyed? You can always just hang up on me . . . Oh, right, we're not on the phone. Then you can just quit reading, I guess.

# I-WONDER PONDERIMS

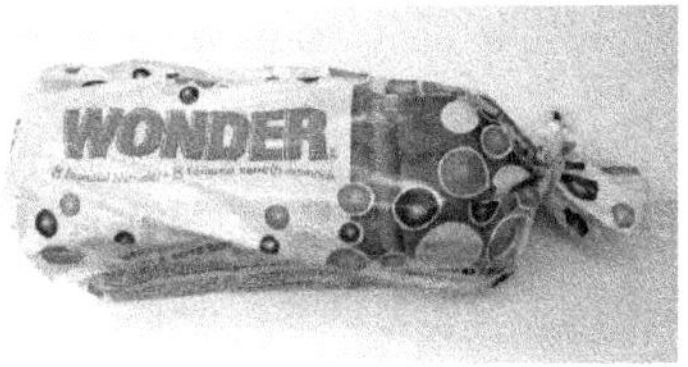


If you have time to ponder, you have time to wonder. Or is that the same thing? I take that with a slice of bread (Wonder bread, of course). Anyway, these are wonderments that I don't have any other category for. So go ponder them.

Can you wish on the same star two nights in a row?

How can you see a bright future if it hasn't happened yet?

What color is a jail bird?

Can you get a close shave with a dull blade?

If someone is nonverbal, does that mean they don't use verbs?

If there is "nothing new under the sun," how did they come up with McDonald's?

Why doesn't phonetics start with an F?

If you ask for nothing and get nothing, would you celebrate?

Can you honk your horn three-and-a-half times?

Can you really stop thinking for a moment?

Well, now I wonder if you understood any of that. Did it make sense? Did it matter in your life? Did it give you indigestion? Did it . . . ? Oh forget it.

## WHAT-IF PONDERISMS

Have you ever wondered what if ? What if you hadn't been born? How would the world have been different? Better? Worse? Or did it not matter?

What if you were rich? Would you benefit the world? Or your community? Or your family? Or yourself? See what what if can do to your own thinking. Read on.

What if you threw yourself to the ground . . . and missed?

What if vegetarians ate meat?

What if God was dead? Who would save the Queen?

What if you starrted out with nothing and still had most of it?

## Jack STARR

What if a synchronized swimmer drowned? Do the rest have to drown?

What if you broke the silence? Could you put it back together?

What if you try to fail and succeed? Which of the two have you done?

What if you got everything you wanted? Where would you put it?

What if Christmas came at a time when the stores weren't so crowded?

What if you solved your parking problems by buying a parked car?

What if my mind got caught in a washing machine? Would that clean up my thoughts? This what if thing could get complicated, confusing, or convicting. I think I will be more decisive in the future.

## "WHO SAID?" PONDERISMS 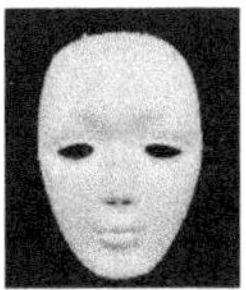

"Who said?" . . . these ponderisms are really an oxymoron. I said them, of course. Or rather, I thought them up. Some are take-offs of other sayings or different ways of saying truths, fiction, life lessons, or really dumb things. I think you will agree with the latter.

Who said . . . ?

"You can't sled uphill."

"There are two sides to every argument: yours and the correct one."

"Men, be assertive. Don't wear an apron when doing the dishes."

"If you can't stand the heat, turn on the air conditioner."

"If yesterday news was so important, why is it lining the bottom of a birdcage?"

"If you were paid what you were worth, there would be no inflation."

"He who laughs last may just be a slow thinker."

"If the shoe fits, get another one just like it."

"What was the best thing *BEFORE* sliced bread?"

I don't think I need to *say* anything more about this.

# Lessons

Life Lessons Ponderisms

Rule To Live By Ponderisms

Life Experience Ponderisms

A Practical Ponderisms

Ponderisms That Offer Solutions

Nonsense Ponderisms

Miscellaneous Ponderisms

Uncategorized Ponderisms

## LIFE-LESSON PONDERISMS

Did you graduate from the school of hard knocks? If so (and you're not inspired to practice those hard knocks on my head) you could probably add to this list.

Some of these are practical, some ridiculous, and some impossible. So if you can't use any of them, just disregard and move on to the next.

The only mistake you can make while sleeping is oversleeping. And you thought you couldn't make a mistake while sleeping.

The best way to lower your golf score is with an eraser.

Life is better with a smile on your face, a song in your heart, and chocolate in your hand.

If you can't change your life, at least change your attitude.

Don’t let tomorrow or yesterday use up much time today.

WOW. How prophetic or pathetic was that? Think you can do better? Send me some and we will see.

## "RULES TO LIVE BY" PONDERISMS *

We all know about the GOLDEN RULE. Well, there are several other rules you probably don't know about, and they make wonderful ponderisms.

The SILVER RULE: Do not do anything that ten years from now you will wish you had not done.

The RUBY RULE: Give unto others the advice you didn't use yourself.

The IRON RULE: Rulers who rule with an iron fist proclaim that 'might makes right.'

Now a couple of these you may not have known about. You can look them up, and good luck with that. BUT PONDER THEM. Think about what they are trying to tell you. Then react accordingly or change your life to fit them . . . even one of them. Parents seem to favor the Iron Rule.

Now ponder why there is no Diamond Rule, Sapphire Rule, or Emerald Rule. At least not ones that you have heard of. Perhaps because they don't exist or are a variant or subset of the Golden Rule.

Or maybe you will write them. Let me know for my next book.

## LIFE EXPERIENCE PONDERISMS

Life throws a lot at us. Sometimes we catch it, sometimes we miss it. But regardless, these lessons are meaningful and often worth a few minutes of our time to ponder them in some detail. DO IT! DO IT NOW!

Will buying time add more minutes to your day?

If you could live your life over, would you ________________? (You can probably fill in that blank way better than I can.)

Is the secret to a good life being content with what you have? Or is more better?

Courage is facing your fears and conquering them.

Living on the edge means staying sharp at all times. What else does living on the edge mean?

With your experience and knowledge, explain what P's and Q's are.

If your life were a story, could you read it out loud in church?

You only live once. So make it happy and lovely; don't screw it up.

Winning and luck do not go together. Winning and preparation do.

Follow your dreams, but only AFTER you wake up.

The secret to a good life is walking in the rain with the one you love.

These are only a few ponderisms involving life experiences. Sometimes they are easy to define and sometimes not. You could probably add many more to each question. I know I have. Why not try that and quit just reading these ponderisms for entertainment?

## A PRACTICAL PONDERISM

Here is a Practical Ponderism that you can use when you are traveling. See if you think it would work.

If you ever worry about falling asleep while driving, put a hundred-dollar bill in your left hand and hold it out the window.

I don't know about you, but that will definitely keep me awake if it's my hundred-dollar bill! See? Some ponderisms have benefits. They are not all stupid or inconsequential.

# PONDERISMS THAT OFFER SOLUTIONS

People want solutions. Here are some that may answer your question, whatever that may be, so use them if appropriate.

Any amount of good advice will not cure the common cold.

Be smart enough to know better and old enough not to care

The two most important words in a bad situation are not “IF ONLY” but rather “NEXT TIME.

If you wait until you are forty for life to begin, you will miss a lot along the way.

Learn from others’ mistakes. You will not live long enough to make them all yourself.

You will never FIND time for everything; you must TAKE time.

Now these do offer some nuggets for living. Feel free to pass them on to others and forget about giving me credit. I probably stole them from someone else anyway. If you think about it, these do offer some good advice for those who take advice. Some take it with a grain of salt, and others with a dose of castor oil. It all comes out in the end, I suppose.

## NONSENSE PONDERISMS

In this category you will find ponderisms that are kooky, impractical, and of no value. However, you can try and make sense of them if you wish. Good luck.

If a hundred-yard dash is one hundred yards long, how long is a dash of pepper?

A college education never hurt anyone who is willing to learn something afterward.

If you think you can, you are right. If you think you can't, you are also right.

If your uncle is worth $100,000 dead or alive, are you from a wealthy family?

If you need a hearing aid but can't afford one, try this. Put a button in your ear and run a thread or string down to your pocket. People will see it and talk louder.

Is a practical nurse one who marries a rich old man?

Is there any pattern or sense out of all of these? If so, please let me know what it is.

# MISCELLANEOUS PONDERISMS

Miscellaneous means that I didn't know in what category to put these. And it means that I haven't thought much about them either. I think I need a vacation.

Try drawing something miscellaneous.

If a cannibal used a knife and fork, would that be considered good manners?

Is it possible to be a little bit pregnant?

If you depend on a rabbit's foot for good luck, remember it didn't help the rabbit.

Why is someone else's good idea just beginners' luck?

Advice is like an enema. Sometimes it is needed, but the person receiving it may not want it.

If you have a lot of irons in the fire, wear asbestos gloves.

The most powerful force in the universe is gossip.

Join the TNT club: TODAY, NOT TOMORROW.

You learn more by paying attention than by asking questions.

Being in this category, you are really not average . . . you are not at the top of the heap either. (Who wants to be top of a heap anyway? Ash heap, heap of garbage, heap of trouble . . . Does anything good ever come in heaps?) You are unique—even if you don't have a specific category. Embrace that.

## UNCATERGORIZED PONDERISMS

These ponderisms do not seem to fit into any categories I have dreamed up, thought up, or written down. They may fit someday in some category not as yet defined, discovered, or invented, but until then they belong here—to these pages, to the ages, to the world, to the universe . . . let's not get carried away here.

Is it possible to be more or less specific?

How can pretty be ugly? Can you be pretty ugly?

Which came first, the ant or the picnic?

Almost anything is easier to get into than to get out of.

Can you use a day bed at night?

What do common ordinary people have in common?

Wow. These are pretty disconnected. Like an unplugged floor lamp. Oh-oh, Watch out, here he goes again.

Adam and Eve were pretty lucky. They did not have to go through puberty.

If only the good die young, does that mean that old people are bad?

Which part of a half-truth are you supposed to believe?

Education teaches us what we don't know. (Now that is something, I think.)

Has your groove turned into a rut?

There probably are more of these, but perhaps in the next book. Don't hold your breath until then.

# Final Thoughts

## HOW DO PONDERISMS EVOLVE?

You are now about to learn "the secret." Don't tell others. Let them figure it out for themselves. Let's show you how ponderisms evolve. Take SELF-RISING FLOUR, for example. Here goes.

How early do you have to get up to beat self-rising flour?

Does self-rising flour need an alarm clock? (See how this goes?)

Does self-rising flour ever fall out of bed?

Does self-rising flour get up before chickens do?

Does self-rising flour go to bed early so it can get up before dawn?

Will self-rising flour rise up above all other foods?

How high does self-rising flour get?

If you punch self-rising flour, it goes down. Does it ever get up again?

There is seemingly no end to how many ponderisms you can make up out of a single phrase. Try it on a topic and see what you can come up with. Or send your ideas to me and let me do the work. You need to think outside the box. Whatever that means. (Is it bad to think inside a box? What if you're thinking, "How do I get out of this box"?)

It is comforting to realize that no one thinks like I do, or else this book would already have been written.

## AFTERTHOUGHTS

Well, there you have, it folks. A whole series of PONDERISMS. I have many, many more, but I will keep them for the second edition. There will be new categories also, and I hope I will not repeat any of these. But if truth be known, you probably wouldn't know if I did or not.

I hope this afforded you some entertainment or that I made you think a little. Look for the next edition, which I know you are patiently awaiting. So am I, but I don't think my publisher is as enthusiastic. At any rate, have a good life, and if you can't do that, have a not-so-bad one.

www.ingramcontent.com/pod-product-compliance
Lightning Source LLC
Chambersburg PA
CBHW070532130626
46555CB00003B/1381
* 9 7 8 1 9 4 5 9 7 5 0 3 5 *